spot

AWESOME NATURE

FLOWERS

by K.C. Kelley

AMICUS

petals

pollen

Look for these words and pictures as you read.

stem

bud

Flowers come in many colors.
Let's spot some flowers!

Flowers grow almost everywhere.
Plants use their flowers
to grow new plants.

bud

Look at the flower bud.
Buds grow into flowers.

petals

See the petals?
The colors look good to bees.
Bees eat the flower's nectar.

pollen

Look at the yellow powder.
It's called pollen.
Pollen makes new flower seeds.

Look at the stem.
It helps the flower stand tall.
Water flows through the stem.

stem

Amber waters her flowers.
What flowers would you grow?

petals

pollen

Did you find?

stem

bud

spot

Amicus Readers and Amicus Ink are imprints of Amicus
P.O. Box 1329, Mankato, MN 56002
www.amicuspublishing.us

Library of Congress Cataloging-in-Publication Data
Names: Kelley, K. C., author.
Title: Flowers / by K.C. Kelley.
Description: Mankato, MN : Amicus, [2018] | Series: Spot. Awesome nature | "Spot is an imprint of Amicus."
Identifiers: LCCN 2017022135 (print) | LCCN 2017033777 (ebook) | ISBN 9781681513270 (pdf) | ISBN 9781681512877 (library binding : alk. paper) | ISBN 9781681522470 (pbk. : alk. paper)
Subjects: LCSH: Flowers--Juvenile literature. | Readers (Primary) | Vocabulary.
Classification: LCC QK653 (ebook) | LCC QK653 .K44 2018 (print) | DDC 582--dc23
LC record available at https://lccn.loc.gov/2017022135

Printed in China

HC 10 9 8 7 6 5 4 3 2 1
PB 10 9 8 7 6 5 4 3 2 1

Megan Peterson, editor
Deb Miner, series designer
Patty Kelley, book designer
Producer/Photo Research:
Shoreline Publishing Group LLC

Photos:
Cover: Lepas/Dreamstim.com.
Inside: Dreamstime.com:
Volkop 1, Raquelbagnol 2tl, Tosca Weijers 2tr, Joanna Waksmundzka 2bl, Hurry 2br, Nutthawit Wiangya 3, Inna Felker 4, Lasse Ansaharju 6, Nicky Jacobs 8, Catiamadio 10, Elena 12. Shutterstock: Lucian Coman 14.